About Alex Gutteridge

I am a woollyback, which means I was born and brought up in Leicestershire. I still live there with my husband, three children, two cats, one hamster and too many fish to count. I love autumn, skipping and fresh raspberries, and I hate feeling cold, anything to do with maths, and spiders.

Pirate Polly sailed into my head during a train journey and she wouldn't go away until I'd written about her.

Coming soon from Alex Gutteridge

WITCH WENDY WORKS HER MAGIC

PRINCESS POSY, KNIGHT IN TRAINING

Pirate Polly
Rules the Waves

Alex Gutteridge

Illustrated by Chambers and Dorsey

MACMILLAN CHILDREN'S BOOKS

First published 2004 by Macmillan Children's Books
a division of Macmillan Publishers Limited
20 New Wharf Road, London N1 9RR
Basingstoke and Oxford
www.panmacmillan.com

Associated companies throughout the world

ISBN 0 330 43304 0

1 3 5 7 9 8 6 4 2

A CIP catalogue record for this book is available from
the British Library.

Typeset by Macmillan Publishers Limited
Printed and bound in Great Britain by Mackays of Chatham plc, Kent

Contents

For my father

Fishy Business

Chapter One

Pirate Polly paced up and down the deck of her ship, the *Glad Tidings*. She nibbled her nails, she twiddled with her hair and she stared out to sea.

"I'll *never* be a proper pirate," she said to Howler, her dog, and Rufus, her rat. "I *still* need to complete three treasure hunts, two desert island rescues and a deed from the Unlucky Dip

before I can take off my L-plates. That will take forever."

"Could you sit down for a minute?" Howler mumbled. "You're rocking the boat and I'm feeling a teeny bit queasy."

"What a wimp," Rufus snorted, rolling his eyes to the sky. "The dopey dog's seasick and we're still in port."

Polly plonked herself on the bare boards and fondled Howler's pointy ears. Waves slapped against the hull of the boat and a monstrous shadow swept over the deck. Howler let out a little whine as a hulking great ship pulled alongside the *Glad Tidings*.

"Are you still here, Pirate Polly?" a big hairy pirate bellowed across the bows. "Why don't you pack in trying to become one of us and go home to your mum?" Mad-Eyed Mick leaned over the edge of the *Fishy Business* and fixed Polly with his most scary glare.

Polly jumped to her feet. Rufus reared up on his hind legs and boxed the air with his forepaws. Howler dived for cover behind Polly's legs.

"Just because I don't have a big bushy beard," Polly shouted.

"Or make a h-horrible, hair-raising noise," Howler stammered.

"Or have a permanent parrot problem," Rufus grunted.

"Just because I'm a bit different," Polly said, trying to stop her legs from wobbling and her voice from shaking, "doesn't mean I won't make a good pirate."

Mad-Eyed Mick threw back his head, clapped his hands together and

laughed like a squad of squabbling
seagulls.

"In your dreams, Pirate Polly," he
guffawed as he steered the *Fishy
Business* to the other side of the
harbour. "Or I'll paint my boat pink!"

"What a cheek!" Howler huffed.

"We'll show *him*!" Rufus said.

"But what if mean old Mick really is right?" Polly sighed. "What if I'm just not up to the job? What if I *never* get enough points to become a fully fledged pirate like the rest of them?"

"Nonsense," Rufus scolded, "you'll make a perfect pirate, won't she, Howler?"

"You'll be wicked," Howler said, nuzzling the back of Polly's knees.

"I'm not sure . . ."

"What we need is another adventure," Rufus said. "We'll go ashore and check the pirates' pinboard. That will give us all the latest news."

9

"On the way there we'll stop at the shops," Howler nodded, "and stock up on essential supplies."

"If you say so," said Polly. "What do you think we need?"

"Let me guess what the crafty canine has in mind," said Rufus. "Dog biscuits?"

"A brilliant idea!" Howler grinned his soppiest grin. "I couldn't have thought of anything better myself."

Chapter Two

Mad-Eyed Mick stormed into the pet shop and slammed the door so hard that everything and everyone shivered and shook. Polly, Howler and Rufus hid behind a swaying display of dog biscuits.

The cross pirate banged on the pet-shop counter with both fists.

"I *need* another parrot today," he shouted, his ebony eyes whirling

wildly in their sockets.

"I–I'm afraid I'm out of parrots,"
stammered Mr Pettit, the pet-shop
owner. "You had the last one
yesterday. I won't have any more for
a couple of weeks. You've had
enough parrots for a whole pack of
pirates. What *do* you do? Eat them?"

Mick licked his lips with his slug-
like tongue and hissed, "You'll get me
into trouble with your pie-in-the-sky
ideas."

"Looks like another parrot's flown
the shoulder," Rufus sniggered.

"Wise old bird," smiled Polly.

"A pirate can't go on a treasure
hunt without a parrot to map-read,"

ranted Mick, "and I'm leaving first thing in the morning."

Polly pricked up her ears and Rufus jumped on to the nearest shelf. He crept closer to Mick.

"L-look," stammered Mr Pettit. "I really can't help you."

Mad-Eyed Mick leaned over the counter and breathed smelly pirate breath all over him. He grabbed the shopkeeper's tie and pulled him closer. Something inside Mr Pettit's shirt pocket let out a terrified tweet.

Mick's eyes gleamed. Mr Pettit's pocket quivered. Mad-Eyed Mick plunged his hand inside and pulled out a small blue bird.

"It's only my pet budgie," said Mr Pettit. "She's not suitable for a pirate at all."

"Is she obedient?" snarled Mick.

"Oh no," said Mr Pettit. "She's still in training."

"Never mind!" Mad-Eyed Mick shrugged. "I'll sort her out. I've had plenty of badly behaved birds."

"Forty-two at the last count," whispered Polly from behind the biscuits.

16

Mad-Eyed Mick cast a sly glance round the room. Polly, Howler and Rufus shrank back into the shadows.

"Does she talk?" Mick snapped.

"Oh no," Mr Pettit protested. "She's not chatty like a parrot."

"Good!" guffawed Mick. "I'm fed up with blabbing birds. I'll take her."

"B-but she's not for sale," Mr Pettit stammered.

"I'll borrow the bird then," Mick growled.

Mr Pettit crossed his fingers behind his back. "She's never even looked at a map," he lied.

Mad-Eyed Mick fixed a small lead anchor to the budgie's leg and plonked

17

the petrified bird on his shoulder. He strode towards the door.

"She'll soon learn to map-read," he snarled. "Or else . . ."

"When will you be back?" Mr Pettit sniffed, wiping a tear from his eye.

Mick paused right next to Rufus. The little rat froze as still as a sugar rodent. Polly held her breath. Howler covered his eyes with a paw.

Mick lifted up his hat and whipped out a packet of puff pastry and a scrap of paper.

"I'll be back as soon as I've found the treasure marked on this map," he grinned, waving the piece of yellow paper above his head.

"This," he smirked, "is the route to the loot, and your budgie is going to help me find it."

The budgie's beady black eyes stared straight into Rufus's prawn-pink ones.

19

"HELP!" she mouthed at him.
"P-please help me!"

Chapter Three

As soon as Mick was out of sight, Polly made a dash for the door.

"Don't worry," she called over her shoulder to Mr Pettit. "We'll go straight to the pirates' pinboard to see if there are any clues to where Mick's heading."

"We'll have the birdnapped budgie back before you know it," Howler said, picking up his bag of biscuits.

"*And* we'll go after the treasure," Rufus added.

The pinboard was empty.

"What's the point of having a noticeboard," Polly huffed, "if the other pirates won't use it properly?"

"Well, that's the end of that," Howler sighed.

"The treasure hunt is cancelled," Polly brooded.

"That bird is definitely doomed," Howler whimpered.

"The project to turn Polly into a proper pirate is doomed too," Polly sighed. She scratched Howler's head. Howler licked her hand.

"I always thought that a delicate dog like me was not really designed for a life on the ocean wave," he mused. "I've often thought I'd make a brilliant basket tester or a talented biscuit taster."

"I've never wanted to be anything other than a pirate," Polly snivelled.

"And you still can be," Rufus promised. "Remember Rule Number Two of *The Buccaneers' Handbook*."

"*Pirates are positive*," Polly replied sulkily.

"So all we need to do is play hide-and-seek . . ."

"Of course," Polly laughed, blinking away her tears. "You are such a clever rat, Rufus."

"Are buried bones involved?" Howler asked, wagging his tail. "Or a nice squeaky toy?"

"I'm talking about hide-and-seek on the high seas, you dim-witted dog," Rufus snapped. "We're going to follow Mad-Eyed Mick."

"All right," Howler said, looking hurt. "There's no need to be quite so ratty!"

"But first we'll go and say goodbye to my mum," said Polly.

Mrs Plum packed a picnic basket. Then she plaited Polly's hair and kissed her twice on each cheek.

"*Do* be careful, dear," she sighed.
"I wish you would find a proper job,
like hairdressing or shopkeeping.
Being a pirate is so da—"

"Dazzling," Polly interrupted, doing
a little twirl.

"No," Mrs Plum replied. "That's
not quite what I meant."

"Daring," Rufus
said, practising his
punches.

"Yes," Mrs Plum murmured, "but I wasn't going to say that."

"D-dangerous?" Howler stammered, his tail shaking like a sail in a gale.

"Exactly," said Mrs Plum. "Which is why it's such a relief to know that you're there, Howler, protecting my Polly."

Howler smiled his bravest smile. Polly gave a quiet snigger, and Rufus rolled on his back and laughed until his whiskers ached.

Chapter Four

It was dark when Polly hurried to the harbour, the picnic basket in one hand and her shiniest spade in the other. Several pirate ships had gathered in the port.

"Uh-oh!" Polly said, pursing her lips.

"Press-Gang Pete must have got wind of the buried treasure," Rufus said.

"I can smell Stinky Dave several strings of sausages away," Howler sniffed. "And he's a lot closer than that. Pooh!"

"We'll never beat these better pirates to the treasure," Polly sighed. "And we haven't even planned the budgie rescue. Perhaps we ought to sneak aboard the *Fishy Business* and find her before Mick sets sail."

Howler felt his nose turn hot and dry. He shook his head so fast he made himself dizzy.

"It's a b-big b-boat," he choked. "The budgie c-could be anywhere. It would t-take hours to f-find her, and Mad-Eyed Mick might find us first."

"The dog's not as dense as he looks," Rufus said. "It might be better to wait."

"If you say so," Polly said, boarding the *Glad Tidings.*

"We do," Howler and Rufus agreed.

Polly pulled up the gangplank and went below deck to put on her pyjamas.

"We'll have to be awake early," Rufus said, setting his alarm clock. "Mick's bound to leave at the crack of dawn."

Polly stared through the porthole into the starry night. Out of the corner of her eye she saw something move. She

31

pressed her face to the glass. A large,
dark shape moved slowly and silently
across the water towards the open sea.

"The sneaky sea serpent," she gasped. "Mad-Eyed Mick's not waiting until the morning. He's leaving now."

Rufus hopped out of his hammock and bounced into Howler's basket.

"Wakey, wakey, you lazy mutt!" he shrieked. "It's all paws on deck. Mad-Eyed Mick's on the move and we've got to sit on his tail."

"Talking of tails," Howler groaned, "you're sitting on mine. Owww!"

A milky moonlight lit up the sky and a brisk wind pestered the clouds.

The *Fishy Business* whipped over the water, followed by the *Glad Tidings*. Once or twice, Polly thought she spied the shapes of other ships hidden by the night, and Howler was sure he heard strange squawking sounds drifting across the water.

As soon as dawn broke, Rufus scrabbled up the main mast to do some pirate-spotting.

"Pirates ahoy!" he called to Polly. "Mad-Eyed Mick's still in sight on the

34

horizon and Press-Gang Pete is sailing
sneakily to starboard."

"Stinky Dave's pong is coming
from all directions," Howler added,
"and it's putting me off my breakfast!"

★

The *Fishy Business* steered to the south, east, north, west and south again.

"I smell a rat," Polly said, studying the chart.

"Didn't you use any soap this morning, Rufus?" Howler frowned.

"What Polly means, you hopeless hound, is that Mick's playing games with us."

"He must have spotted us," Polly sighed.

"No worries," Rufus murmured. "We'll dwindle into the distance."

"Melt into the mist," added Howler.

"Of course! "Polly cheeered. "We just need to make Mick and the others think that they've given us the slip."

"Aye aye! Captain Polly," Howler
and Rufus nodded.

Chapter Five

Mad-Eyed Mick finally dropped anchor in a quiet cove. Polly moored the *Glad Tidings* in the next bay. Press-Gang Pete was nowhere to be seen, and there wasn't the slightest whiff of Stinky Dave on the warm wind.

"This is the perfect place for a picnic," Polly said, gazing at the sandy beach.

"We need to keep an eye on Mick," Rufus said. "We could eat the food on top of that cliff."

"We can look down into the next bay from there," Polly agreed, and she set off for some steps cut out of the rock.

"Come on, dogsbody," Rufus called to Howler. "Don't drag your paws. Pick up that picnic basket. We're hungry!"

"What took you so long?" Rufus asked as Howler panted over to the picnic place.

"The steps are steep, the basket's heavy and —" Howler glanced over

40

the edge of the cliff – "heights make me feel a bit peaky."

Polly opened the basket, kissed Howler on the nose, and offered him a cold sausage.

"Urgent business to attend to first," he gasped. "Back in a minute."

Howler loped over to the nearest tree and started sniffing. He lifted his back leg.

"EXCUSE ME!" Rufus shrieked. "You're not going to wee on *that* tree?"

"Why not?" Howler asked.

"Because you're putting me off my seed cake," Rufus grumbled. "Go away. A long way away."

"All right," Howler huffed. "Keep
your fur on."

He trotted through a thicket of
palm trees, studying each trunk
carefully. At last he found the perfect
tree. He lifted his leg, tilted his head
and closed his eyes.

"Excuse me!" something blue trilled

above him. "You can't wee under this tree."

Howler gritted his teeth and looked up. A small blue bird looked down her beak at him.

"This is a special tree," she explained, fluttering down in front of him.

Howler crossed his legs and studied the bird. "Did you know, you're the chirping image of Mr Pettit's birdnapped budgie?"

"That's me. I've jumped ship. I've escaped the clammy clutches of Mad-Eyed Mick and I've been looking for—"

"Your way home," Howler interrupted. "Don't worry." He grinned a doggy grin. "I am the dog of your dreams. I can give your wings a rest and take you home on the *Glad Tidings*."

"Oh! Thank you very much, but first of all you're not a digging dog as

44

well as a dreamboat, are you?"

"I have got my paws dirty in the past for something really special," Howler said, "like big buried bones."

"What about buried treasure?" whispered the budgie. "Is that special enough for you?"

Chapter Six

"You hopeless hound," Rufus shouted as Howler trotted back to the picnic place. "You've been ages."

"Mad-Eyed Mick has gone," Polly added. "We'll never catch up with him now. It's hopeless. *I'm* hopeless."

"Actually—" Howler started to say.

"That poor little bird." Rufus placed his paw on his chest. "Lost forever.

Mad-Eyed Mick will probably
barbecue it on some lonely beach."

"In fact—" Howler tried again.

"If only you hadn't taken so long,"
Rufus snarled. "We could have chased
after him."

"Not a good idea," a little voice chirped. The budgie landed between Howler's ears. "Mad-Eyed Mick can't read a map for all the barnacles on a boat. He'll be going completely the wrong way."

"I've been trying to tell you," Howler said. "This is Mr Pettit's birdnapped budgie, and she knows where the treasure is."

"Howler!" squealed Polly. "You're a hero!" She threw her arms round his neck.

"I don't believe it!" Rufus groaned.

48

"That just about takes the biscuit!"

"Yes please," Howler grinned.

Polly, Howler and Rufus followed the budgie back through the trees until they reached the right place.

"This is the spot," she trilled.

Polly shovelled, Howler scrabbled and Rufus scratched at the bare earth. The budgie was on birdwatch.

"We must be quick," Polly puffed.

"Mick may be thick," Rufus agreed, "but even he will trace the treasure trail eventually."

"Are you sure this is the right tree?" Polly wheezed as the hole got deeper and deeper.

49

"That budgie looks a bit of a birdbrain to me," Rufus huffed.

"Excuse me," the budgie called crossly. "If *you'd* just escaped a fate worse than being stuffed, your memory might be a bit muddled. That *Fishy Business* is one spooky ship. It's awash with scary sounds that are enough to make your feathers fall out."

"It's probably haunted by the souls of those poor parrots," Howler shivered.

"Pah!" Rufus grizzled. "Twaddle!"

Suddenly, Polly's spade made a clanking sound as it struck something hard.

"I think I've found it," she said, jumping up and down.

"Uh-oh!" sang the budgie. "Pirates approaching. The *Fishy Business* is careering round the cliff. Stinky Dave and Press-Gang Pete are hovering on the horizon."

Polly hauled the treasure chest out of the hole and prised open the lid.

"The *Fishy Business* has dropped anchor," the budgie twittered.

Polly, Howler and Rufus gasped. The chest was full of shiny gold coins.

"Mad-Eyed Mick is looking madder-eyed than ever," the budgie shrieked. "I think it's time to fly."

Chapter Seven

Polly was halfway across the beach on her way back to the *Glad Tidings* when Mad-Eyed Mick scuttled out from behind a rock.

"Polly Play-Pirate!" Mad-Eyed Mick raged. "Give me that treasure."

"Finders keepers!" Rufus called, trying to bite through Mick's boots.

"We'll see about that," Mick said, stamping his foot and creeping closer.

"Howler, do something," Polly
pleaded.

Howler tried his grizzliest growl. It
sounded like a cat purring.

Mick grabbed at Polly's shirt with
one hand and tugged at the treasure
chest with the other.

Howler tried his bravest bark. It
sounded like a mouse squeaking.

"It's *my* treasure," Mick snarled.
"How did you find it?"

"I'm not telling," Polly said,
pursing her lips.

"I bet it was that blessed budgie,"
Mick snarled. "Birds! Can't keep their
beaks shut, any of them. That's why I
had to get rid of the parrots. One

look at a treasure map and they were gossiping all over the place."

Polly shook herself free and backed away. Mad-Eyed Mick lurched after her. "What are we going to do?" the budgie sobbed. "What are we going to do?" Howler groaned.

"Will you stop repeating everything parrot-fashion," Rufus snapped.

Suddenly, his eyes gleamed.

"I've got an idea," he whispered. "Howler, keep close to Mick and look horrible. You should find that easy. Featherhead, show me where the spooky sounds were coming from on Mick's ship."

Rufus skittered across the sand and followed the budgie towards the *Fishy Business*. From the bowels of the boat they heard grumbling and scratching. Rufus gnawed as fast as his teeth would bite until he'd made a skull-sized hole at the edge of the hatch door.

There was an eerie silence, followed quickly by the sound of bad-tempered birds jostling and blinking their way into the daylight.

"There he is!" they cawed. "The pasty-faced pirate who was planning to turn us into a huge parrot pie."

Forty-two parrots exploded into the sky like a firework display, before dive-bombing towards the beach. They smacked Mick in the face with their wings, they clawed tufts from his beard and bit him on his bony bottom.

Mick ran for the trees, shrieking and spitting.

"Remember Rule Number One in *The Buccaneers' Handbook*," Polly called

after him. *"Pirates don't panic."*

Mick turned and stuck his tongue out, only to have it pecked by a parrot.

As the *Glad Tidings* sailed away with a chest full of treasure and a prow packed with parrots, Mad-Eyed Mick picked bird droppings out of his beard.

"That's ten points for a treasure hunt," Rufus shouted.

"A lifetime's supply of dog biscuits for a budgie rescue," Howler called.

"And a feather in my cap for saving

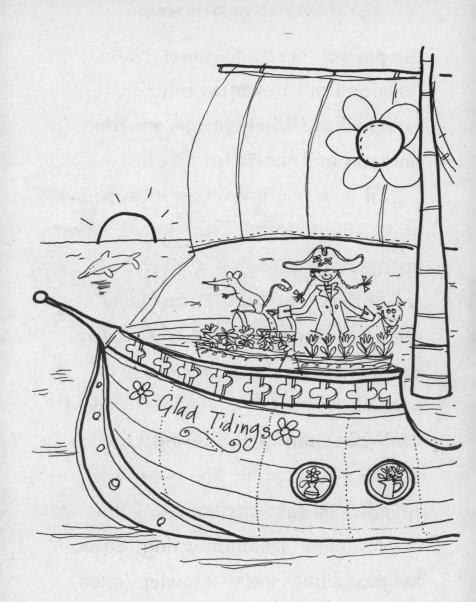

the parrots," Polly laughed. "What have you got to say to that?"

Mad-Eyed Mick peered out from the trees and shook his fists.

"I'll stop you becoming a proper pirate, Pirate Polly," he snarled. "You just wait."

"There's one thing I can't wait for," Polly sighed as the *Glad Tidings* eased her way through the waves towards home.

"What's that?" Rufus and Howler asked.

"After all that excitement, I just can't wait to get home to my mum," laughed Pirate Polly.

Making Waves

Chapter One

Pirate Polly plodded across the deck of her ship, the *Glad Tidings*. She straightened her plaits, picked up her pirate's hat and plonked it on her head.

"Will I *ever* be a proper pirate?" she asked Howler, her dog, and Rufus, her rat. "I *still* need to complete two treasure hunts, two desert-island rescues and choose a

deed from the Unlucky Dip before
I have enough points to take the
L-plates off my boat."

"Which is why we're going to
Captain Flounder's Funfair," Rufus
replied. "Now, are you ready to
tackle the Unlucky Dip?"

"As ready as I'll ever be," said
Polly, trying to sound brave.

"I really don't like funfairs,"
Howler whimpered. "All that
spinning and swinging is not good
for a delicate dog. Can't we try a
desert island rescue instead?"

Polly kissed Howler's cold, wet
nose and stroked his curly coat.

"I'm tempted by a treasure hunt

myself," she whispered, "but—"

"Captain Flounder's Funfair only comes once a year," Rufus said. "Do you really want to wait another twelve months before earning your pirate points from the Unlucky Dip?"

"Yes!" Howler barked.

"No!" Polly cried.

"Well, what are we waiting for?" Rufus asked. "Let's get on with it."

The port was packed with pirate ships. Howler kept close to Polly's heels, while Rufus hung from the brim of her hat.

"Funfair ahoy!" Rufus called. "Pirate party ahead!"

"Oh, my hammering heart!" Howler groaned, winding his tail round Polly's leg. His nose twitched. "Oh, my nervous nostrils, what can I smell?"

"Pirates, you dim-witted dog,"

Rufus scoffed.

"Not just any old pirate," Howler said in a trembly voice. "Surely you can smell him on the wind. It's—"

A huge black boot thumped down on the pavement next to Howler's paw. A dirty, snotty hand clamped down on Polly's shoulder. A smell as vile as the sewers in summer swamped the air. Rufus gulped as Stinky Dave breathed rotten-fish breath in his face.

"You're not heading for the funfair, are you, Pirate Polly?" the squat, spotty pirate hissed menacingly in her ear. "We've told you before, girls don't make good pirates. Why

don't you save everyone a lot of
trouble and hurry back home to
your mum?"

"Oh no," Polly gasped. "I couldn't
do that. I need to do a deed from
the Unlucky Dip and get ten more
points towards my pirate's licence."

Stinky Dave stamped his feet and

spat like a cross camel. "We'll see about that," he huffed before skedaddling away into the crowd.

"Oh dear!" Polly groaned. "I get the feeling this Unlucky Dip could be a hopeless task if Stinky Dave and his pirate pals have anything to do with it."

"In that case," Howler said, perking up, "we might as well give up now and go home for a nice juicy bone."

"Perhaps you're right," Polly sighed.

"Are you a serious seafarer?" hissed Rufus.

"Of course," replied Polly.

"Are you a devoted dog?" Rufus snapped.

"You know I am," Howler huffed.

"Are we going to let a bunch of petty pirates beat us? Can't we outsmart them? Isn't Pirate Polly going to be the best pirate since sliced seed cake?" Rufus yelled.

Polly clenched her fists and squared her shoulders. "You're right, Rufus, as usual," she said, blowing him a kiss. "I can't give up now. Unlucky Dip here we come."

"I wish I wasn't quite so devoted," Howler groaned as he sloped after them.

Chapter Two

Polly stopped just inside the entrance to the funfair. The noise was as deafening as a wailing-walrus party. Howler whimpered and Polly coiled her plaits round her ears.

"Can you see the Unlucky Dip?" she shouted to Rufus.

"I can see the Storm-in-a-Teacup ride," he called. "We could have a go on that."

Howler dropped to the ground and started to whine.

"Over there's the Walk-the-Rotten-Plank game. I like that one too," Rufus said, twitching his whiskers.

Howler buried his face in the back of Polly's plimsolls.

"But what about the Unlucky Dip?" Polly reminded him.

Rufus twizzled round. "Oh yes, there it is, and . . . uh-oh, I predict pirate tricks."

"I knew it," Polly groaned. "What can you see?"

"Stinky Dave, Mad-Eyed Mick and Press-Gang Pete have just crept

out of the Unlucky Dip tent and
they're heading this way," Rufus
said, hopping down
on to the ground.

"Oh, my
petrified paws,"
snivelled Howler.

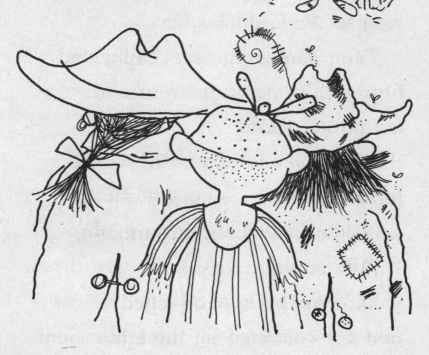

"I told you we should have stayed on the ship."

"Well, if it isn't Pirate Polly with her pathetic pooch and wretched rodent," Mad-Eyed Mick guffawed as he came up to Polly, "on their way to the Unlucky Dip."

"You can't stop me," Polly said firmly. "I'm determined to earn my ten pirate points!"

"We don't intend to stop you." Mad-Eyed Mick's eyes flashed wickedly beneath shaggy eyebrows.

"We thought we'd show you the way," Stinky Dave added, "in case you got distracted by the Ghost-Ship ride or the Win-a-Whale stall."

"How thoughtful," Rufus murmured.

Stinky Dave flashed his most slippery smile and put his arm round Polly's shoulder. There was a sickening smell of sweaty armpit. Polly tried to pull away and Howler wondered whether he dared nip at Stinky Dave's foul feet. He decided he daren't.

"I've heard a rumour the deeds are especially difficult this year," Press-Gang Pete sniggered, grabbing Polly and propelling her through the crowd.

"How very fishy," Rufus murmured.

"You wouldn't have anything to do with that, I suppose?" Polly gulped.

"Us?" The three pirates blinked guiltily. "How could you think that we'd fiddle with the Unlucky Dip?"

"Quite easily," Rufus said to himself.

"Oh dear!" Polly muttered, as she stepped inside the black-and-white striped tent topped with a skull and crossbones. The three pirates stayed outside.

"Do you think I'm about to make a complete fool of myself?" she asked.

"Absolutely," said Howler.

"Not," Rufus added. "The half-baked hound means absolutely not."

"I just know they've done something to this Unlucky Dip to

try to stop me becoming a proper pirate," Polly fretted.

"You could be biting off more than you can chew," Howler warned. "We could be going home with our tails between our legs."

"You'd know all about both of those, greedy guts," Rufus retorted.

"I can't chicken out now," Polly said, grinding her teeth. "I've got to have a go."

Inside, the tent was gloomy and damp and smelt of seaweed. Captain Flounder sat next to the Unlucky Dip. Hidden inside the huge, sawdust-filled barrel were tricky tasks for trainee pirates. The captain had a beard as white as sea spray, skin like a pickled walnut, and a shifty stare. Howler shuddered at the sight of him. Polly plunged her hand into the barrel.

Unlucky Dip

"Dig deep," Rufus urged. "Those pirates are as thick as two short planks. They're bound to have put their deed near the top."

"Good thinking," Polly agreed, pushing down towards the bottom of the barrel. "I've got something," she cried, clasping a piece of paper between her fingertips.

Polly dashed outside with Rufus clinging to her collar. Stinky Dave, Mad-Eyed Mick and Press-Gang Pete were loitering nearby. Their eyes gleamed spitefully as Polly unfolded the paper. She didn't know they'd taken all the tasks out of the barrel and replaced them

with ones of their own.

Polly turned pale.

"Is it bad?" Rufus asked.

"Worse than that," Polly gulped.
"It's dreadful."

"Hooray!" the terrible trio burst out. "Face it, Pirate Polly. You just haven't got what it takes to become a proper pirate."

Chapter Three

Stinky Dave, Mud-Eyed Mick and Press-Gang Pete pranced away, crowing with pleasure. Polly, Howler and Rufus started to make their way back to the *Glad Tidings*.

"Tell us the worst," Rufus said.

"We've got to swap ships with Stinky Dave," Polly replied glumly. "*And* we've got to clean up his wreck of a boat so it's fit to enter

the Spick 'n' Span Pirate Ship
Competition the day after
tomorrow."

"That's terr—" Howler howled.

"Terrific," Rufus interrupted. Polly
and Howler
stared at him
open-mouthed.
"I'm sure we can
do it."

"There's worse
to come,"
Polly
added

tearfully. "To get the ten points towards my pirate's licence, we've got to win first prize." Her tears plopped on to Howler's nose. "It's impossible."

The *Glad Tidings* bobbed up and down at the quayside. Her woodwork gleamed, her brassware glowed and her sails were whiter than white. Further down the quay the *Dirty Work* festered under the hot sun.

"Look at it!" Polly sighed.

"I don't have to," Howler groaned. "My nostrils are numb already and we haven't even boarded the stinking ship yet. I'll probably never be able to sniff out the scent of bones again. We're not *really* going through with this, are we?" He gave Polly one of his pleading puppy-eyed looks.

"Well . . ." Polly mused.

The gangplank rumbled as Stinky Dave bounded on to the *Glad Tidings*.

"Still here then?" the smelly pirate gloated. "The task too difficult for a pretend pirate, is it? Suits me. I told the others I didn't want my ship tarted up so it shines like sea-soaked pebbles and smells like a flower-filled clifftop."

"Well, that's a pity," Polly said, hoping she sounded more confident than she felt, "because that's just what you're going to get."

"In your deepest dreams," replied Stinky Dave, doubling up with laughter. "My ship's the smelliest, dirtiest, most disgusting ship that sails the ocean waves."

"Yuk!" Howler grizzled.

"The *Dirty Work* hasn't been cleaned for over twenty years," Stinky Dave said proudly.

"But we've got a secret weapon." Rufus curled back his lips and champed his teeth together.

Polly raised her eyebrows at

Howler. The dog looked blankly back at Polly.

Stinky Dave shifted from one foot to the other and slid his eyes sideways. "Oh yeah?" he scoffed. "What's that, a sudden streak of spring-cleaning seagulls, a team of mopping mermaids?" He snorted nervously. "No, I know . . . it's the wash-and-go tidal wave."

"Actually," Rufus replied, "it's better than all of those."

"What is it then?" Stinky Dave snarled suspiciously.

"It's not a what, it's a she," Rufus said, winking at Polly, "and you'll find out soon enough."

Polly's mum packed a suitcase full of cleaning cloths. She filled a trolley with bottles and she loaded a basket full of brushes.

"Are you sure it's not breaking any rules from *The Buccanneers' Handbook* if I come and help?" Mrs Plum asked.

Rufus shook his head. "I've double-checked. There's definitely no rule against parents helping out trainee pirates while they're in port."

"Polly is lucky that you're such a reliable rat," Mrs Plum sighed.

Rufus rubbed his cheek against her hand and stuck his tongue out at Howler.

"And Howler is such a hard-working dog," Mrs Plum carried on. "He deserves a little treat." She placed a large bag of multicoloured,

home-baked biscuits in front of him.
Howler looked up at her adoringly.
"It's such a relief to know that
you'll be there guarding the boat
from attack."

"Guarding?" Howler panicked
and dropped a fish-shaped biscuit
at his feet.

"What attack?" Polly asked.

"Well, it's obvious that those cheating pirates aren't going to just let you clean up Stinky Dave's ship without a fight, dear," Polly's mum explained. "They're bound to try some tricks to stop you."

Howler started to tremble. "What sort of tricks? Dirty tricks? Dangerous tricks. Dog-destroying tricks?"

Polly gave him a hug. "It'll be all right," she soothed. "I'm sure it won't be anything serious. Besides, I'm not worried. We've got the bravest sea dog of them all to protect us."

Howler pricked up his ears.
"Really? Do I know him?"

"She means you, biscuit brain,"
Rufus sighed.

"O-oh!" Howler yelped. "I was
afraid of that."

Chapter Four

Pirate Polly picked up the suitcase with one hand and grabbed her Wackiest Water Pistol with the other.

"We'd better make a start on the smelly ship," she sighed.

"The sooner the better, dear," Mrs Plum agreed, tugging at the trolley.

"I'll bring the nose pegs," Rufus added.

"And I'll bring the biscuits," said Howler.

"Oh yes, they're very important equipment," Rufus sneered.

"Special snacks are vital to an underfed dog like myself," Howler replied. "You never know when you're going to need a biscuit."

Stinky Dave was waiting to give them a guided tour of his ship.

"Who's this?" the ponging pirate asked, glaring at Mrs Plum.

"This is my mum," Polly said.

"Mrs Plum is our secret weapon," Rufus added. "There's nothing she doesn't know about tidying and cleaning."

Stinky Dave looked worried. He licked his wobbly blackened teeth and twitched.

"There's nothing in *The Buccanneers' Handbook* to say she can't help us," said Polly stubbornly.

"All right." Stinky Dave held his salt-cracked palms up in the air.

"Keep your prissy plaits on. I was only asking who she is."

The *Dirty Work* was revolting. Its deck was knee deep in rotting banana skins and festering fish bones. Its sails were full of holes, its portholes dripped with slime, its hull was caked in mud and its masts were studded with seagull droppings. Below deck was almost as bad.

"Is it worse than you thought?" Stinky Dave grinned.

"Mmm," replied Polly.

"Brilliant!" Stinky Dave jumped up and down, making sickening squelching sounds on the disgusting deck. "I hope you've left the *Glad Tidings* nice and neat," he said.

"She's as clean as a new fin," Polly replied.

"Excellent," said Stinky Dave. "I've never won the Spick 'n' Span Pirate Ship Competition before."

"I think I know why," Mrs Plum gasped.

"You're not going to enter the *Glad Tidings* in the competition, are you?" Polly pleaded.

"Of course," Stinky Dave grinned. "If you can enter my boat, I can enter yours."

"But that's not fair," Polly protested.

"Worst of luck, Pirate Polly," Stinky Dave guffawed, slithering down the gangplank, "although you don't need it. You'll never clean up this boat in time, even with the help of your mum."

★

Polly scrubbed the sails and Mrs Plum mended the holes with brightly coloured pieces of patchwork. Rufus scraped away the seagull droppings and Howler swept the deck until his tail ached.

"It's looking better," Polly said at the end of the first day.

"It certainly smells better," Rufus added.

"If I have to sweep up anything else I'll go completely bananas," Howler grumbled.

"At least we haven't had any interruptions from pirates," Mrs Plum said thankfully.

"Perhaps they're not going to be

quite so horrible to me after all," Polly murmured.

"And fish might fly," Rufus added.

Mrs Plum unpacked the sleeping bags from her trolley. "We need an early start tomorrow to get this finished for the competition," she yawned.

"We'd better sleep on deck tonight," Polly said. "It's still a bit dirty and smelly down below."

"But it will be dark," Howler whined.

"The moon and the stars will give some light," Mrs Plum soothed.

"It'll be cold," Howler shivered.

"We'll snuggle up together,"
Polly said, cuddling him.

"I wish I was a lapdog, living the
life of luxury, instead of roughing it
on a beastly boat."

"And I wish you'd stop moaning,
or you'll end up being a dog
overboard if I have my way," Rufus
snapped.

"Shh!" Polly lay down, making
sure her water pistol lay next to her.

"Everything will seem better in
the morning," added Mrs Plum.

Chapter Five

Howler couldn't sleep. Deep
shadows lurked all over the boat.
He closed his eyes and tried
counting bones. It made him feel
hungry. Between Rufus's snores he
thought he heard strange splashing
sounds. Howler squeezed his eyes
shut even tighter and pictured
himself scaring seagulls and chasing
after driftwood.

Something banged softly against
the side of the boat. Howler's eyes
snapped open. He pricked up his
ears and wiggled
his nose. He
thought he heard
wild whispering,
but he *knew* he
could smell
something nasty
on the breeze.
He felt a trembling in
his tummy, a looseness in his legs
and a quiver down his tail. The
smell got stronger, the whispering
got louder and there was a
scraping and tapping against the

115

hull of the *Dirty Work*.

"Oh no!" Howler whined. "Oh help!"

He licked Polly on the cheek and nudged Rufus with his nose. "Wake up!" he pleaded. "I think we're under attack."

Rufus sat up, sniffed and scrambled on to Polly's shoulder. "Pirates paying a visit," he whispered in her ear, "and I don't think they've come for a friendly midnight feast."

Polly grabbed her water pistol and woke up her mum. "Hide," she commanded. "Hurry!"

★

Polly, her mum, Howler and Rufus
crouched behind some barrels.
Something smelly landed with a thud
next to them on the deck, followed
by the sound of muffled laughter.

"Ready?" Polly said.

"Steady," Rufus added.

"No-o-o," Howler groaned.

Polly, Rufus and Mrs Plum lunged forwards. Stinky Dave, Mad-Eyed Mick and Press-Gang Pete were hanging on to the side of the boat with one hand and throwing reeking rubbish on to the deck with the other.

"I can see you, you plotting pirates," Polly cried. "Take this!"

She fired her water pistol straight at their faces, just as Rufus sank his teeth into Press-Gang Pete's thumb and Mrs Plum jammed a bucket over Mad-Eyed Mick's head.

"I can't see!" spluttered Mick.

"Ugh!" wailed Stinky Dave. "I hate having my face washed."

"I can't swim," Press-Gang Pete yelled as he fell into the water.

"Serves you right," Mrs Plum shouted as the pirates jumped to Pete's rescue and hauled him into a little rowing boat to disappear into the darkness.

"What a mess!" Polly groaned, stepping over manky milk cartons and piles of stinking seaweed. "Even if we get this cleared up, we'll never have time to spruce up the outside of the boat before the competition."

"Of course we will," Rufus said as brightly as he could. "We'll think of a way."

"Thank goodness Howler was on lookout duty," Mrs Plum sighed. "He's such a wonderful watchdog."

"Talking of the hapless hero," Rufus coughed, "where is he?"

Howler poked his head out from around a barrel. "Is it safe to come out?" he whispered. "Have they gone?"

"For now," Polly said, kissing his nose. "Did you sense danger, Howler? Is that why you stayed awake?"

"Absolutely," Howler nodded. "I felt it in my bones."

"More likely you couldn't get to sleep because you're afraid of the dark," Rufus scoffed.

"What a thing to say," said Howler in a pained voice.

"So where *were* you when all the trouble was happening? Biting your claws behind a barrel. That's hardly the behaviour of a great guard dog," Rufus sneered.

"I was guarding my biscuits, of course," Howler said. "Besides, all that squirting and spraying leaves a dog feeling totally washed out!"

Rufus stared at Howler in amazement. "You are the drippiest dog I've ever met," he said, "but you've just given me a dazzling idea."

an that.

g

ute

,

ven

,,

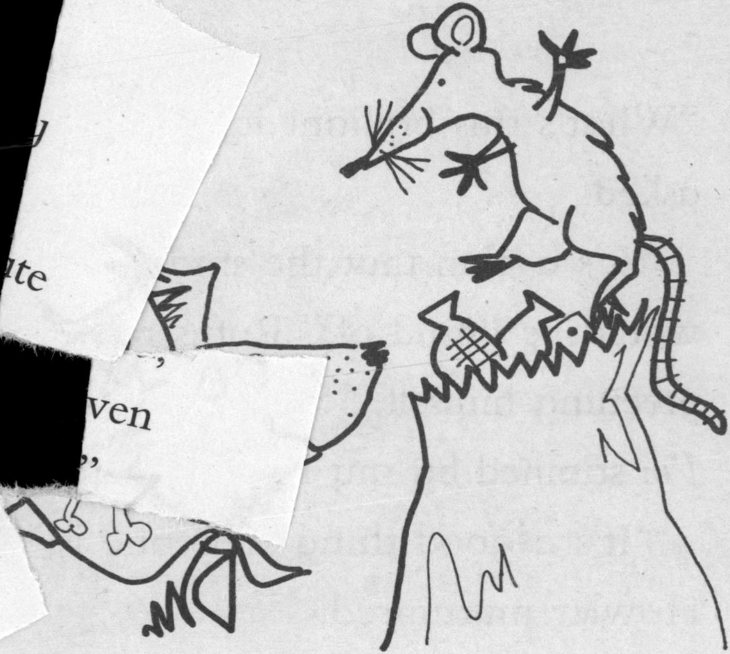

"What's this brilliant idea?" Polly asked.

"It's a plan that the smartest pir[...] would be proud of," Rufus replied, preening himself. "Sometimes e[...] *I'm* stunned by my intelligence.[...]

"It's a good thing someone is," Howler murmured.

"So tell us what to do," Mrs Plum said.

"First, we have to clean through the night," Rufus instructed. "Then we need to sail the *Dirty Work* across the harbour so it's as near as possible to the *Glad Tidings*."

"But once the judges see the two boats next to each other the *Glad Tidings* is bound to win the competition," Polly frowned. "Then I won't get any pirate points."

"Not necessarily," Rufus smiled.

"Won't Stinky Dave make fun of us?" Polly's mum asked. "Won't the other pirates jeer and laugh?"

"I *do* hope so," Rufus said in a mysterious voice. "But, trust me, it will be worth it."

125

★

"I can't believe you're going along with the rat's ridiculous plan when he won't even tell us what it is," Howler grumbled as they all sprayed and swept and polished the *Dirty Work* above deck and below.

"It's got to be worth a try," Polly whispered. "I know one thing. If it doesn't work, we're sunk."

"Where are the lifeboats?" Howler looked around, panic-stricken.

"I mean that I won't stand a chance of getting my pirate points," Polly said.

"Phew!" Howler sighed. "That's a relief. Well, in one way it is and one way it isn't. *You* know what I mean."

"Just keep that tail moving," Polly smiled.

By dawn the *Dirty Work* almost looked presentable.

"There's still the hull to clean," Polly's mum sighed. "Above the water-line it's caked with mud and seaweed and stray candyfloss from the funfair."

"The judges will be here by breakfast time," Polly fretted.

"Let's pay Stinky Dave a visit,"

Rufus suggested with a grin, "and put the plan into action."

Polly manoeuvred the *Dirty Work* across the water.

"It's such a lovely-looking boat," she sighed as they got nearer to the *Glad Tidings*.

"It *was* such a lovely-looking boat," Polly's mum gasped, "before Stinky Dave got his filthy hands on it."

Polly blinked. Her mouth fell open. Her eyes filled with tears. The *Glad Tidings* looked terrible. The deck was littered with unwashed plates, biscuit wrappers and snotty tissues.

"It's rather smelly," Howler sniffed. "I hope Stinky Dave's parrot hasn't done anything nasty in my basket."

"What's happened to my beautiful boat?" Polly cried. She stormed up and down the deck and waved her fists in the air. "It's ruined," she sobbed.

"Totally wrecked," Rufus agreed. "I don't think he should get away with such bad behaviour, do you?"

"No, I don't," Polly shouted, getting more and more cross. She grabbed her water pistol and charged to the edge of the boat.

"Oh dear," Howler whined,

tugging at the top of Polly's sock. "Don't do anything rash. You know Stinky Dave is rather trigger-happy when he's annoyed."

Polly was too angry to listen.

"Stinky Dave, you good-for-nothing, first-class slob of a seafarer, come out here and explain what you've done to my beloved boat," she yelled.

"This isn't like Pirate Polly. She's such a sweet-tempered pirate normally. Can't *you* stop her?" Howler pleaded with Mrs Plum.

Polly's mum shook her head.

Stinky Dave slouched on to the deck of the *Glad Tidings*.

"Uh-oh," Howler whimpered. "Here we go."

"You've turned my boat into a rubbish dump," Polly shouted.

"And *you've* turned the *Dirty Work* into a picture-postcard pirate ship," Stinky Dave spat. "It'll take me weeks to turn it back into a grot-spot."

"You didn't think we'd clean it up as well as we have, did you?" Mrs Plum laughed.

"If you weren't such a pig of a pirate, we'd have completed the job ages ago," Rufus said scornfully.

Stinky Dave snorted and rocked from side to side.

"You've done it now," Howler said, closing his eyes.

"That's the general idea," Rufus whispered.

Stinky Dave leaned down and picked up his Super Soaker. He pointed it at the *Dirty Work* and fired. He missed Polly and hit the hull.

"Some pirates are so predictable!" Rufus jumped up and down. "The Reliable Rufus Plan is under way."

He scrabbled up a rope and whispered something in Mrs Plum's ear. She nodded and took the wheel.

Polly pointed her Wackiest Water Pistol at Stinky Dave and shot back. The force of the blast knocked his

hat from his head. Rufus and Mrs
Plum cheered. Mad-Eyed Mick and
Press-Gang Pete whizzed up on deck
and aimed their Super Soakers at
Polly. They missed her and hit two
portholes just above the water-line.

"Can someone
keep this boat
still?" Polly
shouted.

Mrs Plum slowly turned the *Dirty Work* full circle and the pirates soaked the other side of the ship with their wayward shots.

"I'm trying, dear," she replied apologetically, "but you know I'm a bit like a fish out of water when it comes to anything technical."

Chapter Seven

"You can stop now," Rufus shouted.

"Why?" Polly asked, ducking an unusually well-aimed shot from Stinky Dave.

"Why?" bellowed the three pirates, banging their heads together as they tried to avoid a splattering from Polly's pistol.

"Because our mission is accomplished," Rufus laughed. "The

Dirty Work is as bright as a white polar bear, thanks to you three and your feeble sense of direction."

Polly looked at the boat. It was true. The pirates' aim had been so bad that their water pistols had washed the whole hull clean.

"See you at the judging," Polly shouted.

"You'll never win," Stinky Dave blared.

"You've cheated," Mad-Eyed Mick yelled, rolling his eyes.

"We'll get you for this," said Press-Gang Pete, stamping his foot.

"What this boat needs now is a homely touch," Mrs Plum mused as Polly moved the *Dirty Work* across the harbour. "We haven't got time to go out and buy flowers and candles, but some decorations would make all the difference."

There was a slurping and gnashing sound coming from behind a barrel. Rufus's eyes lit up. He raced towards the sound and whisked a sandcastle-shaped biscuit out of Howler's mouth.

"No more of those for you, fat face," he said. "I've got a far more important job for these biscuits than filling your belly."

"What can be more important than that?" Howler complained. Polly, Rufus and Mrs Plum pegged the dog biscuits around the *Dirty Work*.

"I hope you know this is the ultimate sacrifice for a desperately hungry dog," Howler moaned.

"You can eat them once the judges have finished," Polly said.

"Shh, here they come. Stand up straight and smile."

The *Dirty Work* was the last ship

to be inspected. The judges ran their fingers over her woodwork, and admired their reflections in her gleaming glass portholes, and they wrote lots of notes in their big black books. They didn't smile once. Polly felt her heart sink into her plimsolls.

"That's it, we've lost," she whispered.

Everyone gathered by the harbour steps to hear the results.

Stinky Dave shuffled backwards and forwards in his holey boots.

"And the winner of the Spick 'n' Span Pirate Ship Competiton for this year," the judge announced, "is . . ."

Polly put her hands over her ears.

". . . and I can't believe I'm actually saying this," the judge carried on, "the winner is the *Dirty Work*, for being the tidiest, cleanest ship in port, and for having the most imaginative decorations."

"It's not fair," shrieked Stinky Dave. "It must be fixed!"

"We've done it." Rufus hopped up and down on Polly's shoulder and yelled down her earhole.

"I told you," said Howler, grinning at Rufus. "You never know when you're going to need a biscuit."

Polly couldn't wait to spruce up

the *Glad Tidings*.

"Phew," she sighed, dumping the last banana skin in the bin. "I think that'll do. A bit of sea-salty air-freshener and you'd never know that Stinky Dave had been here."

Stinky Dave peered over the edge of the soap-scented *Dirty Work*. His nose was clamped with clothes pegs.

"You've been lucky, Pirate Polly, but you've still got to complete two treasure hunts and two desert-island rescues, and they're not easy-peasy lemon-sole squeezy. You're still a long way from being a proper pirate. It's time for you to face that fact."

"I know what it *is* time for," Polly giggled as she gathered up her basket of bottles.

"Tea, fishcakes, some of my biscuits?" said Howler hopefully.

"It's time to go home with my mum," smiled Pirate Polly.

Going Overboard

Chapter One

Pirate Polly twirled across the deck of her ship, the *Glad Tidings*. She flung out her arms, threw back her head and laughed.

"Soon, I'll be a proper pirate." She smiled at Rufus, her rat, and Howler, her dog. "I *only* need to complete two treasure hunts and two desert-island rescues, *then* I can take the L-plates off my boat."

"Hooray!" Rufus shouted, jumping up in the air.

"I wish we were on the same wavelength," Howler whined.

"All the other pirates will have to treat me like a serious seafarer when I'm properly qualified, won't they, Rufus?" Polly asked.

"Hmm." Rufus frowned. "I suppose so."

"They'll have to stop being mean," Polly chuckled.

"And nasty," Howler added.

"And ganging up on me." Polly grinned.

"I don't think you should get your hopes too high," Rufus murmured.

"Talking of pirates," Polly said, glancing nervously around the harbour, "look out, here they come!"

Mad-Eyed Mick marched along the harbour wall, whistling tunelessly. A plastic parrot sat on one shoulder and a big net was draped over the other.

"Can't you find a real feathered friend?" Rufus taunted.

"Pah!" Mad-Eyed Mick spat.

"Why have you bought a new fishing net?" Polly asked.

"It's not a fishing net," Mick guffawed, "it's a . . . um . . . er . . . hammock. I'm going to find a nice quiet spot to relax."

"That's the oddest hammock I've ever seen," Polly said to Rufus as Mick pulled-up the gangplank to the *Fishy Business* and prepared to set sail.

"Hmm, very peculiar." Rufus frowned. "He must be sickening for something."

"Talking of sickening," Howler gulped, "smell that."

Stinky Dave squelched past the *Glad Tidings* on the way to his ship, the *Dirty Work*. He was twizzling a shiny new compass from the end of a disgustingly dirty finger.

"Where are you going with that compass?" Polly asked suspiciously.

"Nowhere special," Dave smirked. "I thought I'd go and um . . . er . . . gather some seaweed for a face pack. A pirate can't be too careful about his skin." Stinky Dave patted his crusty cheek.

"That's incredible," Polly said, raising her eyebrows as Stinky Dave leaped aboard the *Dirty Work* and set off for the open sea.

"Don't you mean unbelievable?" Rufus said. "And now here comes Press-Gang Pete. He's in a hurry."

"Going somewhere nice?" Polly called as Pete galloped past the *Glad Tidings* with a flashy new lamp attached to the front of his hat.

"Um . . . er . . . What did you say?" Pete stopped and stared at Polly.

"I wondered if you'd got a boat to catch," Polly giggled. "You seem in a bit of a hurry."

"Going . . . er . . . swimming," Pete grunted.

"Why do you need that light on your hat?" Polly asked.

"So I can see under water of course," Pete said, "to . . . um . . . admire all the pretty little fish."

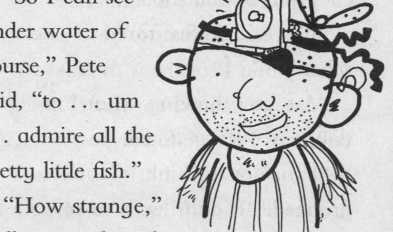

"How strange," Polly gasped as the pirate boarded his ship, the *Jolly Bodger*. "I never knew Pete had a sensitive side."

"I'll tell you what is strange." Rufus frowned. "Press-Gang Pete can't swim."

"Have I ever told you that I once won a prize for the doggy-paddle?" Howler grinned. "It was a treasure chest full of dog food."

Polly and Rufus stared at each other.

"Are you thinking what I'm thinking?" Polly asked.

"I try not to think," Howler groaned. "It only leads to trouble."

"Those pirates were play-acting." Rufus stamped his foot.

"Exactly." Polly nodded.

"And a large net, a new compass and a bright lamp add up to something suspicious," Rufus said, pricking up his ears . . .

"They certainly do." Polly nodded again.

"We'll take the wind out of

their sails," Rufus shouted. "Let's follow them."

"I told you thinking leads to trouble," Howler said, shaking his head, "but nobody ever listens to me."

Chapter Two

"Anchors away!" Polly cried.

"Aye aye! Captain Polly," Rufus saluted.

"Perhaps we ought to check the weather forecast before we leave," Howler pleaded. "There could be a ship-sinking storm on the horizon."

"The sky's as clear as a jellyfish," Rufus scoffed.

"Perhaps we ought to buy in

extra supplies," Howler begged. "Pirates and their crew sail better on a full stomach."

"The galley cupboards are packed as tightly as a tin of sardines," Rufus said.

"Shouldn't we at least say goodbye to Mrs Plum?" Howler whimpered.

"Yes," Polly agreed. "You're right, Howler. We're the politest pirates on the high seas. We must go and say goodbye to my mum."

"Please be careful, dear." Mrs Plum frowned. "I do worry about you. The sea is so . . ."

"Wet?" Howler whimpered.

"You should feel totally at home there," Rufus jeered.

"Unpredictable," Mrs Plum corrected. "I know you have Rufus, who is a first-rate rat, and Howler, who is a dedicated dog, but I can't help fretting. Will you go to bed on time, brush your teeth at least twice a day and make sure you eat properly?"

"Yes, Mum," Polly sighed.

Mrs Plum went to a cupboard.

"I want you to have these," she said. "This was Grandpa Plum's cherished lantern and his finest fishing rod."

"I've got the moon and the stars
to give me light," Polly said, "and I
won't have time to go fishing."

Mrs Plum put her arm round
Polly and kissed her cheek.

"Those mean men might try
something naughty now you're so
nearly a qualified pirate. You could
be stranded without food or need to
signal for help."

"I need help now," Howler
howled. "I'm just an ordinary
biscuit-loving, landlubber sort
of a dog."

Polly blew Howler a kiss and
took the lantern and the fishing rod.

"Don't worry, Mum," she

reassured her. "We'll discover what those pesky pirates are up to, grab some pirate points and be back safe and sound before you know it."

Polly, Howler and Rufus raced back to the *Glad Tidings*.

"Now, which way did that pack of pirates go?" Polly puffed as she scanned the horizon with her telescope.

"I think it was that way," Rufus said, waving an arm towards a large expanse of open sea.

"I thought it was more that way," Polly said, pointing in a slightly different direction.

"It was due west," Howler
groaned.

"Are you sure?" Polly asked.

"Positive," Howler replied.

"How on earth does a
directionless dog like you know
that?" Rufus scoffed.

"I always keep my bag of biscuits
facing east, so they get the morning

sun," Howler replied in a miffed voice. "That way they are nice and warm for breakfast. Stinky Dave definitely set off in the opposite direction."

"Howler, you are so clever." Polly clapped her hands together. "Isn't he amazing, Rufus?"

"Absolutely astonishing," Rufus said with a weak smile.

Chapter Three

The *Glad Tidings* headed west with her sails billowing.

At lunchtime Rufus scrambled to the top of the main mast and looked around.

"Can you see anyone yet?" Polly called.

"Not a single sole," Rufus shouted. "I told you not to trust the dotty dog. Now we're all at sea."

"Talk about stating the obvious," Howler grumbled.

"I mean we're lost," Rufus said. "We've been sailing all morning and we haven't spotted so much as a plastic parrot."

"Can't you smell pirates on the wind?" Polly asked Howler.

He stood up on his hind legs and sniffed.

"Ugh!" Howler sneezed. "Now you mention it I can smell windy pirates. We must be getting closer."

"I think you're trying to bluff your way out of a spot of bother," Rufus called down.

"What's that then?" Howler said,

170

squinting into the distance.

"I don't believe it," Polly giggled. "There's Press-Gang Pete."

"I don't believe it either," Rufus groaned. "I was convinced the dog was barking mad."

Polly kept the *Jolly Bodger* just within her sights for the rest of the day.

By late afternoon land loomed on the horizon and the *Jolly Bodger* headed straight towards the shore.

Polly guided the *Glad Tidings* between the rocks and through the shallower waters.

"We'll run aground," Howler howled.

"Will you stop whingeing," Rufus snapped. "Polly's a natural when it comes to navigating."

As dusk fell the *Jolly Bodger* dropped anchor.

"I have the feeling Press–Gang Pete may have spotted us," Polly said.

"He's probably just settling down for the night," Rufus reassured her.

"But if he has twigged that we're trailing him," Polly sighed, "we'll

172

never find out what the terrible trio are up to and I do *need* some more pirate points soon."

"We'll set up a night watch," Rufus decided, "in case he makes a bolt for it under cover of darkness."

Howler drew the shortest dog biscuit and got the first shift.

"Can I have a light on?" he asked.

"Sorry, Howler." Polly stroked his head. "We don't want to draw attention to ourselves."

"Can I have something to munch on?" Howler asked.

"Definitely not," Rufus interrupted. "A dog with a tummy full of treats is a dozy dog."

Howler padded up and down the deck. Every slap of the waves made him jump. Each whistle of the wind made him tremble. Every creak of the boat made him want to dash below deck to where Polly and Rufus were snoozing happily in their hammocks. He scoured the bare boards for a comforting biscuit crumb. There wasn't anything to be found. He stared across the deep, dark water into the distance. He had a sinking feeling in his tummy.

A light flashed once, twice, three times. Howler scrabbled down to Polly and licked her ear.

"There's a light, in the distance," he whispered.

"It's the moon," Polly murmured.

"It's bright, very bright," Howler persisted.

"It's probably the Dog Star," Polly groaned.

"That's very kind of you," Howler said, "but . . ."

"She means the brightest star in the sky," Rufus added, "not the

dippiest dog in the fleet."

"There's no need to be rude,"
Howler huffed. "I'm only doing my
job. I thought you'd want to be

enlightened. I won't disturb you again. I've got the message."

Rufus shot bolt upright in his hammock.

Polly opened both eyes.

"Someone is sending a message," they both said at the same time.

"Howler," Polly said, wrapping her arms round his neck. "Have I ever told you that you are an indispensable dog?"

"I don't think so," Howler mumbled. "Does it mean I get my biscuits now?"

Chapter Four

Polly, Rufus and Howler scrambled on to the deck and peered into the darkness. Polly studied the intermittent flashes of light and tried to remember what *The Buccaneers' Handbook* said about Coarse Code.

"It's Press-Gang Pete," she muttered. "He's trying to contact Mad-Eyed Mick and Stinky Dave. He says, 'Followed by that prize-

winning problem of a pirate, Pirate Polly. Tried to lead her into shallow water. Plan went a bit wrong. Am stuck on a sandbank. Will have to wait for high tide. Meet you at Dead End Cave at midday instead of breakfast time. Don't share out the treasure until I get there.'"

"The good-for-nothing pirate," Rufus exclaimed. "Lucky for us he's a sloppy sailor or we'd be grounded too."

"There's no reply," Polly said, scanning the night sky.

"Do you think we could have a bit of light now?" Howler pleaded. "I've never been the sort of dog that likes being kept in the dark."

"Press-Gang Pete's signalling again," Rufus said.

"I wish someone would reply, then perhaps we could have a bit of light around here," Howler whimpered. He picked up Grandpa Plum's lantern between his teeth and swung it backwards and forwards.

Polly started to smile.

"*We* could pretend to be Stinky Dave and Press-Gang Pete," she said.

Rufus began to chuckle.

"You are turning into a pedigree pirate," he replied proudly.

"Howler," Polly cooed, "have I ever told you that you are a masterly pirate's mate?"

"I don't think you have," Howler said, wagging his tail, "but every dog has his day."

Polly lit Grandpa Plum's lantern and held it above her head.

"What shall I say?"

182

"Tell old pilchard face that we've received and understood his message and we'll take good care of the treasure," Rufus snorted.

Polly stifled a giggle as she began to signal.

"I'll study the charts," Rufus added, "and see how close we are to Dead End Cave."

"I can answer that already," Howler said, shivering. "Too close for comfort."

Chapter Five

Just before dawn the *Glad Tidings* sneaked past the *Jolly Bodger* on her way to Dead End Cave. Press-Gang Pete was asleep in his deckchair, snoring so hard his teeth rattled in their gums and his hat had fallen over his eyes.

"We've got to get there before breakfast," Polly whispered to Rufus as he studied the charts, "or

Mad-Eyed Mick and Stinky Dave
will beat us to the treasure."

"No problem," Rufus replied.
"Mad-Eyed Mick's map-reading skills
are next to useless and Stinky Dave's
charts are always covered in blobs of
food. They're impossible to read."

"It's not a very nice name."
Howler quivered. "I wish it was
called Alive and Well Cave or Safe
and Sound Cave. That would make
me feel much happier."

"It's not meant to sound
welcoming," Rufus groaned. "The
whole point is to keep people
away."

"Well, it hasn't worked with us,
has it?" Howler grumbled.

"Only because I need the pirate
points from finding hidden treasure,"
Polly explained. "I think it's called
Dead End Cave because there's
only one way in and out."

"So, it's not because you go in

186

and don't come out alive?" Howler asked.

"No," Polly said.

"There won't be any skeletons from perished pirates?" Howler asked.

"There'll be bones from a perishing dog if you don't shut up," Rufus snapped.

"All right, all right," Howler huffed. "Don't get your tail in a twist. I was only asking."

Dead End Cave was tucked away between some high cliffs.

The choppy waves drove the *Glad Tidings* towards the rocks.

"Are you sure this is wise?"
Howler asked, as Polly struggled to
steer the ship through the cave
entrance. "I know I'm not the
brainiest dog on the high seas, but
it looks rather dangerous."

The *Glad Tidings* slipped through
the narrow gap in the cliffs.

"You do know that caves are
damp and dark and echoey,"
Howler said. His voice bounced off
the walls and raced around the cave.

"Shh!" Rufus tutted.
"Can't you keep quiet
for once? We need to
listen for sounds of
other pirates. We don't

want to sail into a trap."

"Oh, my poor paws," Howler groaned. "My throat has lost its bark, my legs have lost their balance and my tail has definitely lost its wag."

The water slapped against the rocky sides of the cave as the *Glad Tidings* sailed deeper and deeper into the darkness. Howler clamped his paws over his eyes as scary shadows danced over the deck.

Rufus listened carefully.

"I can't hear anything suspicious," he whispered. "It's time to track down this treasure."

Polly lit her Grandpa's lamp and directed the glow around the rocks. A bat flew straight towards her; she ducked and Howler whined.

"I told you this was a bad place – there's flying mice," he growled.

Polly shone the lamp into every nook and cranny. There wasn't a sign of any treasure.

"There's nothing here," she said at last. "It must have been a trick."

Polly sank to her knees.

"This cave is as empty as . . ."

"A dinnerless dog," Howler said.

"Trying to become a proper pirate is as hopeless as . . ." Polly sobbed.

Glad Tidings

"Crunching a sea-soaked biscuit,"
Howler added sympathetically.

"I bet Press-Gang Pete and the
others are laughing their stripy socks
off," Polly cried.

"The rats," Howler growled. "No
offence," he said to Rufus.

"They've really gone overboard

with this trick," Rufus said.

Howler peered down at the murky water.

"They must have sunk to the bottom if they have," he said.

"What I mean, you drippy dog, is that those pesky pirates have gone too far this time," Rufus explained.

"Oh! Thank goodness for that," Howler gasped. "For an awful moment I thought that dark shape under the water might be a poor, passed-away pirate."

Polly wiped the tears from her eyes and lowered the lamp down to the water.

"Howler," she said, hugging him tightly, "you are a darling dog."

"Well." Howler grinned. "I am a bit of a softie at heart. I wouldn't want anything really bad to happen to those pirates."

"No, no, no!" Rufus said, gritting his teeth. "What Polly means is that you have struck gold."

"Have I?" Howler looked blank.

"The treasure," Rufus said, leaning over the side of the *Glad Tidings*, "is obviously under water."

"And somehow," Polly murmured, "someone's got to get it out of there."

Chapter Six

Howler peered over the edge of the
Glad Tidings and shuddered.

"It looks cold and deep and wet,"
he whined. "Take my advice, it'll
be impossible to fish it out."

"Oh my goodness!" Rufus
exclaimed. "The infuriating dog has
done it again."

Polly clasped her hands together.
"Of course! What do you go

fishing with? Grandpa Plum's fantastic fishing rod."

"Why can't I just keep my mouth shut?" Howler groaned. "Then we might have turned tail and gone home."

Polly dangled the rod over the side of the boat and wiggled the end about in the water. Rufus perched on the edge and shouted instructions.

"Right a little, left a little, down a bit."

"It's no good," Polly sighed. "I can't do it. Someone must go in the water."

Howler started to shake and his

tail started to tremble.

"I have never, ever, in my wildest dreams, wanted to be a dogfish," he grizzled.

"I'll put my swimming costume on," Polly said.

"There isn't time," Rufus replied. "Mad-Eyed Mick and Stinky Dave are bound to be here any minute now."

Howler swung round in a panic to look at the clock. His tail lashed backwards and forwards uncontrollably, skimmed the edge of the boat and knocked Rufus straight into the water.

"Aah!" squealed the little rat as

he fell through the air.

"Oops!" Howler squirmed.

Splash! And Rufus belly-flopped into the water.

"You stupid dog!" he gurgled when he surfaced for air. "What do you think I am, a water rat?"

"Sorry," Howler said. "I thought all rats were good swimmers, but you do look a bit out of your depth down there."

"Rats are good at everything," Rufus spluttered. "Rats are superior to dogs in every way you could think of."

"In that case," Howler said, "while you're there you might as

well make yourself useful and hook
up that line to the treasure chest."

As Polly hauled the rusty old chest
on to the deck of the *Glad Tidings*,
Rufus shivered inside a fluffy towel.

"You look just
like a drowned
rat." Howler
grinned.

"You still look like a dim-witted dog," Rufus snarled.

"Stop scrapping, you two," Polly said. "Look at this lovely treasure chest." She clapped her hands, and the sound echoed around the cave like a round of applause.

"All we've got to do now is get out of here before Mad-Eyed Mick and Stinky Dave turn up," Rufus said between chattering teeth. "I suggest we make a quick getaway."

Chapter Seven

As the *Glad Tidings* slid towards the mouth of the cave, two cantankerous voices could be heard above the sound of the waves.

"I want to go first," Stinky Dave shouted.

"Well, you can't," Mad-Eyed Mick shouted back. "My ship's bigger than yours, so I ought to go first, so there."

"That's not
fair," Stinky Dave
screeched. "It's all your fault that
we got lost."

"Oh no," Polly gasped. "Now
we're in trouble . . ."

She steered the *Glad Tidings* straight
for the entrance and swept out
between the other two pirate ships.

"Pirate Polly!" both pirates
shouted. "What are you doing here?"

"Oh, this and that," Polly
giggled. "Gathering seaweed,
looking for somewhere shady to
string up my hammock, doing a bit
of deep-sea fishing."

Mad-Eyed Mick winked at Stinky Dave.

"There's nothing in that cave that would interest you."

"Absolutely not." Stinky Dave smirked. "It's smelly and dark and empty."

"It is now," Rufus sniggered.

"What are *you* doing here then?" Polly asked.

"Just mooching about," Mad-Eyed Mick replied, stroking his plastic parrot.

"Just stretching our sails," Stinky Dave added.

"Have you come across Press-Gang Pete?" Mad-Eyed Mick asked.

"The last time I saw him," said Polly, "he was stuck for something to do. I'm sure he'll catch up with you later. Have a nice day anyway," Polly shouted, and the *Glad Tidings* sailed off into the distance, leaving Mad-eyed Mick and Stinky Dave staring suspiciously after her.

★

Once they were a safe distance from the cave, Polly, Howler and Rufus prised open the treasure chest. It was full of large cream and pink pearls.

"I think this calls for a celebration breakfast." Howler smiled.

"How about hot chocolate all round?" Polly asked.

"With frothy cream?" Rufus said, licking his lips.

"And biscuits," Howler said, sitting up and begging.

"Of course," Polly laughed.

"Perhaps we'd better check on Press-Gang Pete," Polly said as she

steered the *Glad Tidings* homewards
and dunked a biscuit in her
chocolate.

"I expect the numbskull pirate is on
his way to Dead End Cave," Rufus
said as he licked cream off his nose.

"Or perhaps not," Howler said,
flattening his ears against a horrible
wailing sound.

"Help!" Press-Gang Pete yelled as
the *Glad Tidings* sailed past. "Won't
you take pity on a poor stranded
pirate?"

"No!" Rufus shouted.

"You must be joking," Howler
growled, daring to look Press-Gang
Pete in the eye.

"I'm still stuck fast!" Press-Gang Pete yelled. "I may be here for years."

"Good," Rufus yelled.

"Serves you right!" Howler added, shrinking behind Polly's legs.

"Throw us a rope, Pete," Polly shouted.

"You're not going to help him, are you?" Howler gasped.

"He's probably trying to trick you," Rufus added.

"I don't think so," Polly said. "Besides, if I get Press-Gang Pete off this sandbank it may count as a desert-island rescue."

"Then you'll only have two tasks to perform before you become a fully fledged pirate." Rufus clapped his paws.

"Precisely," Polly said, catching the end of Press-Gang Pete's rope.

"When you're a proper pirate, will we still have to undertake awesome adventures?" Howler asked.

"I hope so," Polly replied.

"And will we have to go to those

pongy pirate meetings to find out the latest news?"

"Well, yes," Polly replied, "that's one of the perks of being a proper pirate. You get to know what's going on *and* you get a discount at the Whole Sailors' Warehouse."

"Does that mean more dog food?" Howler asked.

"Probably," Polly replied, tying the rope to a mast.

"I may be able to cope with being a pirate's dog after all," Howler mused.

The *Glad Tidings* pulled the *Jolly Bodger* into deeper waters.

"By the way," Polly called to Press-Gang Pete, "I stole past Mad-Eyed Mick and Stinky Dave as I was leaving Dead End Cave. They were wondering where you were."

"But I told them I was going to be late," Pete said. He narrowed his eyes. "What were you doing there, Polly Pruneface?"

"Just trying to gain a few more pirate points," she giggled. "I got this flash of inspiration in the night."

Press-Gang Pete stamped up and down on the deck of the *Jolly Bodger*.

"You've got our treasure!" he shouted.

"And I'll get some extra pirate points for pulling you off that sandbank," she replied. "I'm very nearly a proper pirate now, Press-Gang Pete, and when I am you'll have to tell me all the tricks of the trade."

"It won't sink in, will it?" Press-Gang Pete pouted. "We don't want a namby-pamby girl pirate messing up our gang. You should be at home with your mum. Why won't you ever listen?"

"You're right," Polly said, throwing back the rope.

"What are you saying?" Howler and Rufus gasped.

"I'm saying, full speed ahead,"
Polly laughed. "Let's hurry home.
I've got the perfect present for
my mum."

A selected list of titles available from Macmillan Children's Books

The prices shown below are correct at the time of going to press. However, Macmillan Publishers reserves the right to show new retail prices on covers which may differ from those previously advertised.

All Pan Macmillan titles can be ordered from our website, www.panmacmillan.com, or from your local bookshop and are also available by post from:

**Bookpost,
PO Box 29, Douglas, Isle of Man IM99 1BQ**

Credit cards accepted. For details:
Telephone: 01624 836000
Fax: 01624 670923
E-mail: bookshop@enterprise.net
www.bookpost.co.uk

Free postage and packing in the United Kingdom